For Francesco
1982 – 2006

Banana Patch Press
www.bananapatchpress.com

Library of Congress Control Number: 2006906227

ISBN-10: 0-9715333-2-6
ISBN-13: 978-0-9715333-2-5

Printed in Hong Kong

Goodnight
Hawaiian Moon

by

Dr. Carolan

illustrated by

Joanna F. Carolan

It's time for bed in my little grass shack.

The sky outside is turning black.

The tiki torches are burning bright

And the Hawaiian Moon is full tonight.

The palms that shaded me from the sun

Are resting now, their work is done.

The surf dogs are done for the day.

Their surfboards are dry and put away.

The hula kitties dancing is pau*.
*(pronounced "pow", Hawaiian word meaning finished)

They're all curled up without a meow.

The paniolo horse with the flower lei,

Is fast asleep on a bed of hay.

The chicks that pecked at everything,

Are tucked under their mother's wing.

The hermit crabs that crawled around,

Are in their shells, safe and sound.

The turtle that played in the waves,

Is slumbering in an underwater cave.

The dolphins jumping in the sea,

Are drifting together peacefully.

The hibiscus were open and bright,

And now are closed up for the night.

The nene that flew overhead,

Have settled into their grassy bed.

The geckos have eaten their fill,

And are dozing on the window sill.

I'm snug in bed in my little grass shack.

The sky outside is very black.

The tiki torches are no longer alight...

And the Hawaiian Moon
Wishes everyone... Goodnight!

Brahms' Lullaby

E mālie mai 'oe, Kau iho ke keha.
Maluhia ka pō, I ka māhinahina.

E hi'olani nō 'oe, A he moe 'olu ho'i.
A pili hou mai kāua, A wehe kaiao.

Lullaby and good night.
The moon's glowing bright.
Close your eyes, rest your head,
Dreaming snug in your bed.

Good night, lullaby.
While the moon shines in the sky,
Warm tradewinds soothe your rest,
In Hawai'i so blessed.

E mālie mai 'oe, Kau iho ke keha.
Maluhia ka pō, I ka māhinahina.

E hi'olani nō 'oe, A he moe 'olu ho'i.
A pili hou mai kāua, A wehe kaiao.

A pili hou mai kāua, A wehe kaiao.

Hawaiian Lyrics to Brahms' Lullaby

Written by Mālia 'A. K. Rogers

E mālie mai 'oe	*Be still*
Kau iho ke keha	*Rest your head*
Maluhia ka pō	*Peaceful is the night*
I ka māhinahina	*In the pale moonlight*
E hi'olani nō 'oe	*Go to sleep*
A he moe 'olu ho'i	*Pleasant dreams*
A pili hou mai kāua	*Until we are together again*
A wehe kaiao	*In the dawn of a new day*

MĀLIA 'A. K. ROGERS

Mālia 'A. K. Rogers lives on Kaua'i with her husband and 3 children. She has been a teacher in the Hawaiian Immersion Program at Kapa'a Elementary School for 13 years. Mālia currently sits on the Board of Directors for the 'Aha Pūnana Leo, Hawaiian medium pre-schools.

About the READ ALONG CD:

Read by: Amy Hānaialiʻi Gilliom
Brahms' Lullaby performed by: Amy Hānaialiʻi Gilliom
Slack Key Guitar: Ken Emerson

Executive Producer: Banana Patch Press
Music and Sound Design Produced by Michael Ruff
Recorded, Mixed and Mastered by Michael Ruff on Kauaʻi, Hawaiʻi
www.michaelruff.com

AMY HĀNAIALIʻI GILLIOM

GRAMMY® Award Nominee for Best
Hawaiian Music Album, Amy Hānaialiʻi
Gilliom is one of Hawaii's shining stars.
She has won numerous "Na Hoku
Hanohano" Awards, and was named
"Female Vocalist of the Year" in 2000.
A talented entertainer and songwriter,
Amy has won the hearts of many with
her resurrection of Haʻi (female falsetto
singing). For more information about
Amy Hānaialiʻi Gilliom visit:
www.amyhanaialiigilliom.com

KEN EMERSON

Ken Emerson infuses style and soul into
his traditional slack key and steel guitar
compositions. He has been entertaining
listeners around the world with his
unique style for over 30 years. Recipient
of the prestigious "Kahili" Award for
perpetuating Hawaiian culture, Ken is
also a contributing artist and composer on
the first "Best Hawaiian Music Album" to
win a GRAMMY® Award in 2005. For more
information about Ken Emerson visit:
www.kenemerson.com

DR. CAROLAN was born in Melbourne, Australia. He is a pediatrician in private practice on the island of Kaua'i, Hawai'i. He is married to Joanna F. Carolan.

JOANNA F. CAROLAN was born in San Francisco, California. She is an artist and owner of Banana Patch Studio, an art studio and gallery on Kaua'i.

Other Dr. Carolan books available from Banana Patch Press:

> ***Ten Days in Hawaii, A Counting Book***
> ***B is for Beach, An Alphabet Book***
> ***Where Are My Slippers? A Book of Colors***
> ***Old Makana Had A Taro Farm***

Dr. Carolan and Joanna Carolan would like to thank:
  Amy Hanaiali'i Gilliom, Ken Emerson, Michael Ruff, Malia 'A. K. Rogers
  All the keiki in Dr. Carolan's practice.
  Dr. Carolan's staff: Lisa, Laura and Ku'ulei.
  Dr. Carolan's sons: Sean, Seumas, Brendan and Eamonn.
  The Banana Patch team: Sheri, Dennis, Jana, Vicki, Naomi, Mitzi, Angela, Brooks,
  Shanelle, Erin, Michelle, Patty, Liselle, Crystal, Anna, Patricia, Melissa and Alice.
  Tom Niblick of Printmaker in Lihu'e, Kaua'i.

For more information visit:
www.bananapatchpress.com
www.bananapatchstudio.com